Hats!

Kevin Luthardt

For Wilkin.

Thank you, Jesus, my Lord and Savior.—K.L.

Library of Congress Cataloging-in-Publication Data is available from the Library of Congress.

Text and illustrations copyright © 2004 by Kevin Luthardt.
Published in 2004 by Albert Whitman & Company, 6340 Oakton Street, Morton Grove, Illinois 60053-2723.
Published simultaneously in Canada by Fitzhenry & Whiteside, Markham, Ontario.

The design is by Kevin Luthardt and Carol Gildar.
For more information about Albert Whitman & Company, please visit our web site at www.albertwhitman.com.

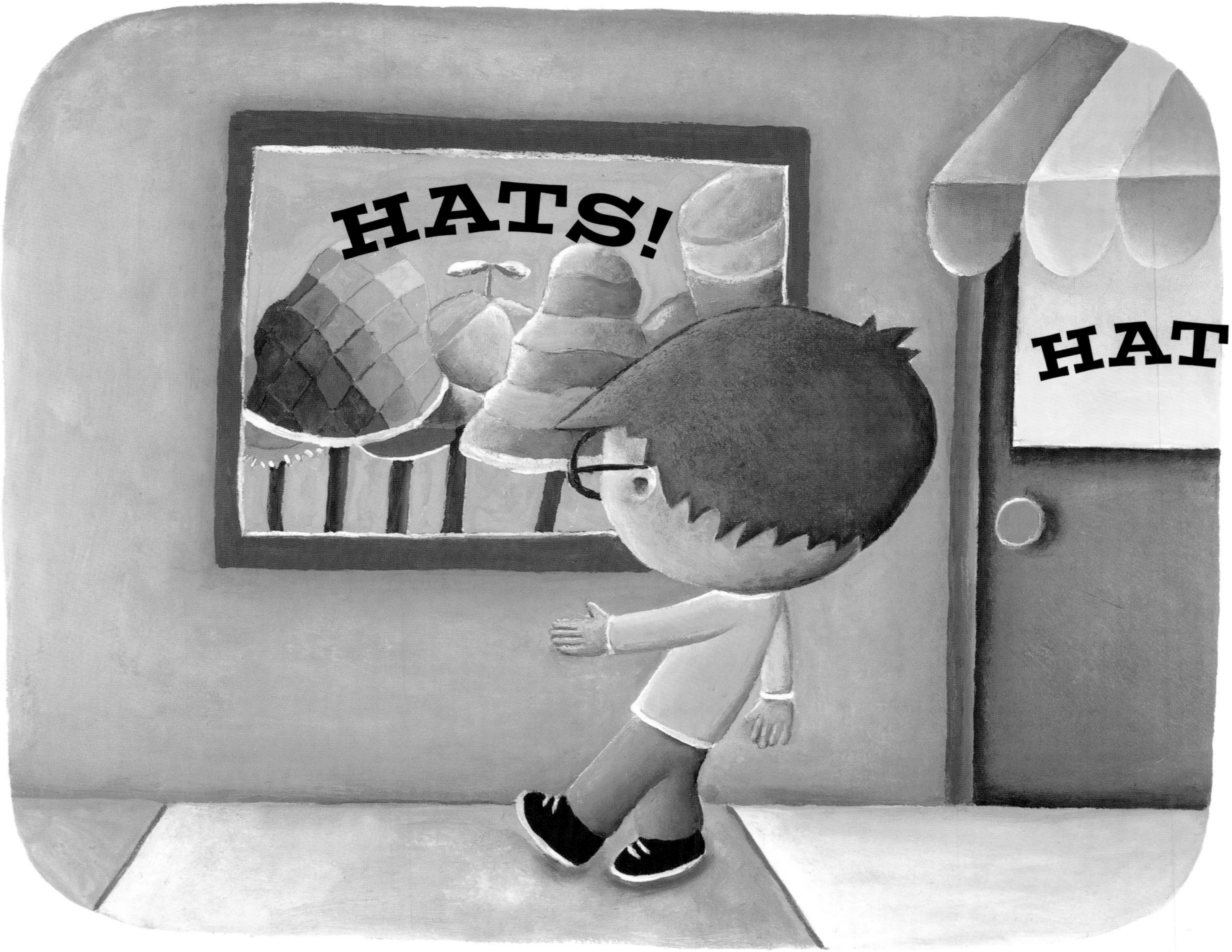
HATS!
HAT